INDIANA JONES

and the

LAST CRUSADE™

**Based on the Motion Picture
Indiana Jones and the Last Crusade**

Directed by Steven Spielberg
Based on a screenplay by Jeffrey Boam
From a story by George Lucas and Menno Meyjes
Adaptation by Les Martin

Random House 🏠 New York

Library of Congress Cataloging-in-Publication Data:
Martin, Les, 1934– . Indiana Jones and the last crusade : based on the
motion picture / story by George Lucas ; screenplay by Jeffrey Boam
and Barry Watson ; adaptation by Les Martin. p. cm. SUMMARY:
Indiana Jones tries to save his father from the Nazis as they all search
for the Holy Grail. ISBN: 0-394-84594-8 (trade); 0-394-94594-8
(lib. bdg.) [1. Adventure and adventurers—Fiction] I. Lucas, George.
II. Boam, Jeffrey. III. Watson, Barry. IV. Title. PZ7.M36353Im 1989
[Fic]—dc19   89-3609

Manufactured in the United States of America   1 2 3 4 5 6 7 8 9 10

Chapter 1

Nobody would dream of calling Indiana Jones a Boy Scout. But he was one once—in the wilds of Utah, where Boy Scouts rode on horses, and the rough-and-ready archaeologist's career of adventure began.

Even then, Indy wasn't exactly your ordinary Boy Scout. He wore a belt woven by native Hopi Indians instead of regulation leather. And he was a lot more interested in breaking new trails and making fresh discoveries than in winning the merit badges in the Boy Scout manual. Indy never did believe in going by the book.

That was why one day he broke away from his troop to explore a cave below a huge rock formation. He was going on a hunch he might find something not in the history books. Tagging along with him was a kid called Herman, a sad sack of a Scout whom Indy had befriended.

Usually Herman followed Indy like a puppy. But today, as they stood before the cave mouth, he had his doubts.

"Why go into this creepy place?" he protested. "Just because your dad is keen on hunting for weird things from the olden days doesn't mean you have to be."

"My dad's being an archaeologist has nothing to do with it," Indy responded angrily. "I just like old places and things—and I like puzzles just as much. That rope leading down to this cave was put here by *some*one. And it must be for *some*thing. I'm going to find out who and what. Course, if you don't want to come along . . ."

"Aw, it's not that," Herman said as they entered the cave. "But—"

"Pipe down," Indy whispered. He saw light from a kerosene lantern dancing in the darkness up ahead. The boys tiptoed toward it, carefully keeping outside the rim of the flickering circle of light.

They saw four men clustering around a recently dug-up hole. Indy recognized it as an ancient burial site. Then he focused on the graverobbers' leader. Indy admired the leather jacket and brown felt fedora hat the man wore. But that was forgotten when he saw what was in the man's hand—a gold cross studded with jewels.

"The Cross of Coronado!" Indy whispered. "Cortés gave it to him in 1520! It proves that Cortés sent Coronado in search of the Seven Cities of Gold."

"How do you know stuff like that?" asked Herman.

"No time to explain," Indy whispered. "Quick. Get back to the troop. Tell the scoutmaster that thieves are grabbing a valuable relic. It belongs to the museum."

"And you?" asked Herman.

"I'm staying here and stopping them," said Indy.

"But how?"

"I'll think of something. Now scat."

"I can't just leave you—" Herman started to argue. Then a snake slithered over his hand. He froze, until Indy calmly brushed the reptile away.

"Be seeing you," Herman said, and headed for daylight.

Indy shrugged. Imagine being scared of a

little old snake! Snakes didn't bother *him*. What bothered him were crooks grabbing relics of the past. It was like erasing part of the memory of all humankind. It made Indy mad.

Indy saw that the man in the fedora had laid the Cross aside to join the others in hunting more loot. Quick and quiet as a cat, Indy crept forward. His hand closed over the Cross. Suddenly something dropped on the back of his hand—an evil-looking black scorpion!

Instantly Indy shook it off. But when he did, the Cross clattered against a rock. The looters wheeled around.

"The Cross!" shouted one of them. "He's got it!"

"Get *him!*" commanded the man in the fedora.

But Indy was already running for the exit. Outside, he hauled himself hand-over-hand up the rope that had led him down to the cave. Reaching the top, he raced along a shelf of rock until he stood directly above where he had left his horse. He remembered a scene from a silent movie he had seen the week before: a cowboy jumping from a rooftop onto his horse and galloping away. It seemed like a good idea. Indy made the leap.

"Oops," he said as he landed in the dirt. His

horse had moved at just the wrong time. He picked himself up and dusted off the seat of his pants. "Guess things work smoother in the movies. But anyway, there's still time for my getaway."

He went to his horse, who was eying him curiously. He swung himself up into the saddle and gave the horse a gentle kick. That was all the horse needed to start racing, and Indy relaxed. His horse was as fast as they came. He'd put plenty of daylight between him and his pursuers.

But this was 1912. Newfangled cars could go faster than any horse. Behind him Indy heard the roar of motors drowning out the pounding hoofbeats. He looked over his shoulder. The crooks had not one car but two. They were bouncing over the desert after him and gaining.

Indy urged his horse on. No use. The cars caught up with him, one on each side sandwiching him in.

A car door opened. The man in the fedora edged out onto the running board, gauged the distance, then jumped onto the back of Indy's horse.

At the same moment Indy made a leap of his own, right onto the top of the car.

The man in the fedora leaped after him, only to have Indy jump back onto his horse. As the cars slowed to let their leader get back inside, Indy's horse regained the lead.

"Not bad, kid, but we'll get you yet!" the man in the fedora yelled as the cars speeded up again.

"Not if I can help it, buster," Indy muttered as he looked for a way out.

He saw it. In front of him were train tracks. A train was barreling down them. If only Indy could—

He could, and did. He raced alongside the train and jumped for it. He made it, going right through the open window of a passenger car—and landing on something very soft.

◆　　　◆　　　◆

Indy blinked, and blushed. He was lying in the lap of a lady—a very loud lady who weighed about four hundred pounds.

"Sorry, ma'am," Indy said to the screaming woman as he hastily got off her lap. He looked around. Gazing at him were midgets, dwarfs, pinheads, a bearded lady, and a rubber man. Indy remembered hearing that the circus was coming to town. He was getting a preview.

Then the door to the train car opened. The

man in the fedora and his gang entered. And Indy was back in his very own three-ring circus. As he raced for the door at the other end of the car, he felt like a kid on a flying trapeze—with no safety net.

He felt even more like one when he made it into the next train car. He got in by climbing an iron ladder and going through a trapdoor in the top. Inside he found himself on a narrow catwalk. Indy looked down and wished he hadn't. He stared into the open tops of vat after vat of live and hungry crocodiles, alligators, giant reptiles, and countless hissing snakes.

"Biggest reptile show on earth," he said to himself as he edged along the catwalk. "But I think I'll give it a miss when it hits town."

Suddenly Indy heard a couple of thumps and felt the catwalk shake. He looked behind him. Two of the crooks had followed him through the trapdoor. They saw Indy and started after him. Then they looked down and froze.

Indy froze too when he felt the catwalk collapsing under too much sudden weight. The crooks were closer to the trapdoor than he was. They were able to make it to safety. Indy couldn't.

Indy wasn't the kid on the flying trapeze

anymore. He was a kid lying on the reptile-car floor. And he was looking up at a giant anaconda boa constrictor rearing over him.

He wiggled away from its crushing coils. He got to his feet, backed away from the boa—and went backward over the side of the biggest vat in the car.

Ughh! Indy was covered with snakes. All kinds of snakes. Slimy snakes. Slithering snakes. Snakes poking into his nose, ears, eyes, mouth. *Ughh!*

Indy desperately kicked at the side of the vat. It broke open. He and the snakes came tumbling out. Lying flat on his face, he saw a sliding door on the train-car floor. It must have been made for cleaning out the car. Indy used it to get him clean out of this jam.

The trouble was, the crooks were still sticking on his trail. With the help of a tiger in one car, a rhino in another, and his own fast feet, fists, and wits, he kept out of their clutches. But they finally cornered him on the top of a swaying stock car.

Racing away from two of them, he bumped into another coming from the opposite direction. Knocked off balance, Indy fell through an opening in the top of the car.

"At least this one is empty," he said to himself, brushing off sawdust. Then he said, "Uh-oh."

A massive shape in the corner rose. And roared.

An African lion. King of the beasts. And it didn't like anyone invading its kingdom.

Even worse, Indy saw the Cross glittering at the lion's feet. It had been sent flying from Indy's pocket when he had hit the floor.

"Nice kitty," Indy said. The lion answered with a snarl of rage.

"So much for sweet talk," said Indy, looking around for help. He saw something coiled on a wall. For a sick moment, he thought it was another snake. Then he saw that it was a trainer's whip. Indy grabbed it.

"Here goes nothing," he said, and lashed out with it.

He managed to hit himself in the chin. But he didn't have time to feel the sting or wonder if it would leave a scar. By now the lion's growl sounded like thunder.

"Guess there's some skill involved," Indy said to himself. "Let's see if I can pick it up."

He tried again. The whip cracked in the air like a pistol shot. The lion backed off a step.

"Keen," said Indy, and cracked the whip again. With a few more cracks of the whip, the lion was backed against a far wall. The Cross was back in Indy's pocket. And he now had a new skill that he intended to sharpen in the future.

That was, if he had a future. Indy still had to get out of this lion's den.

"You got just one way out," a voice called from above. "Toss me the whip, kid."

Indy looked up. The man in the fedora was looking down at him through the opening in the stock-car roof.

"Not on your life!" Indy shouted back.

The man grinned. "You mean, not on *your* life."

Indy saw that the lion was watching him. That lion would watch and wait until—

Indy shrugged. He tossed one end of the whip up to the man.

"Good thinking, kid," the man in the fedora said as he reeled the whip in, pulling Indy to safety.

"You've got heart, kid," the man said as Indy lay panting on the top of the car. "But the cross you have belongs to me."

"It belongs to Coronado," Indy said.

"Coronado's dead, and so will you be, if you keep being stubborn," said the man in the fedora.

12

"Yeah, kid, fork it over," said one of the crooks by his side.

The crook made a grab for the Cross in Indy's clenched hand. A tug-of-war started—and suddenly ended.

"*Awwwk!*" the crook screamed. A snake had crawled out of Indy's sleeve and wrapped itself around the crook's wrist. The crook leaped back, violently trying to brush it off—and Indy saw his chance.

In a flash he was through another crook's legs and dashing for the next car.

But the man in the fedora wasn't worried. "You wait here—so the kid can't double back," he told his men. "I'll go get him myself. He's in the last car. The caboose. He's got nowhere to go. And nowhere to hide."

The man in the fedora entered the caboose in time to see Indy diving into a big black box at one end.

"Nice try, kid," the man said. "But the game's over. Come out with your hands up and the Cross in your hand."

No answer. The man in the fedora shrugged, and moved to take the box apart. Without warning, at his first touch, the box collapsed.

There was no one inside.

The man now knew what kind of box Indy had disappeared into. A magician's trick box.

The trick was on the man in the fedora. He felt a breeze on his back and turned to see the rear door of the caboose swinging open. He ran to it and peered out. Indy was running away down the tracks.

"The kid doesn't know when he's beaten," he muttered.

◆　　　◆　　　◆

Indy felt beat when he made it back home. His legs were aching and his heart was pounding. He headed straight for his father's study. His father was at his desk, copying information from an ancient manuscript into his notebook. Indy gasped out, "Dad!"

His dad didn't look up. "Out! I'm busy."

"But this is really important," Indy protested.

"*This* is more important," his father replied. He indicated a picture painted on the manuscript—some kind of stained-glass window. Despite himself, Indy felt curiosity stirring. He looked closer. There were a bunch of Roman numerals on it. Maybe some kind of code.

"It was lost for nine hundred years," his dad said. "I'm the only one in the world who can make sense of it."

But Indy couldn't forget the problems of the

present. "Dad, I was out with the Scout troop and—"

His father still didn't look up. *"Junior,"* he said, "I suggest you count up to twenty. First in English. Then in Greek."

"But—" Indy began, and saw it was no use. If his father had to choose between Indy and his work, Indy knew who'd come in second. *"One,"* Indy said angrily. *"Two. Three. Four."*

That was as far as he got. He heard a car pulling up outside. His dad kept working. Indy sighed and left the study. If trouble was coming, he'd have to face it alone.

Herman came running in through the un-locked front door.

"I brought him, Indy!" he said proudly.

Behind him came a man wearing a big silver badge.

"Sheriff!" Indy said eagerly. "There were a bunch of them. They almost got me, but—"

"Easy does it, son," the sheriff said soothingly. "You still have the Cross?"

"Yes sir," Indy said. He pulled it out.

"Let's see it," the sheriff said, and Indy handed it over. "Well, no damage that I can spot. I'm sure the rightful owner won't press charges against you."

"What owner? What charges?" Indy asked.

He got his answer when the man in the fedora came in.

The sheriff gave the man the Cross, which instantly disappeared into a leather pouch on the man's belt.

"A fool stunt, son, running off with it in front of this gentleman and his friends," the sheriff said. "Why, your mom would turn over in her grave."

"Boys will be boys, Sheriff," the man in the fedora said. "No harm done. All's well that ends well."

"You two are in cahoots!" Indy said.

"It's not smart to make charges you can't prove," the sheriff said. There was menace in his voice.

"Let him be," the man in the fedora said. "The kid's got spunk. I take my hat off to him."

The man's actions matched his words. He took off his brown felt fedora and placed it on Indy's head.

"Something to remember me by, kid," the man said.

"I'll remember you, all right," Indy vowed as he watched the man and the sheriff saunter off, snickering. "Believe me, no matter how long it takes or how far I have to go, I won't forget you—or the Cross."

Chapter 2

OVER TWENTY-FIVE YEARS LATER, THAT BROWN fedora hat was on Indy's head as he faced the man who used to own it.

That man was wearing a Panama hat now. But the amused expression on his face was the same.

"You never learn, kid," he said. "But I guess I can't call you 'kid' anymore. You're a professor now, I hear. I have to call you 'Dr. Jones.'" His smile widened as Indy struggled in the grip of two burly sailors. They were on the deck of a storm-tossed cargo ship off the coast of Brazil.

"Once again, Dr. Jones, I have to take back my property from you," the man said.

"It's not yours. It belongs in a museum," Indy said.

"Still the same line," the man said as he removed the Cross of Coronado from Indy's belt. "This time, though, I can't let you go. You're a grownup now. You have to pay the full penalty for theft on the high seas. We've got no plank for you to walk. But we can make do without one."

He barked an order to the sailors. They dragged Indy toward the ship's railing.

They didn't make it. Indy's foot lashed out to kick open a clamp holding a bundle of oil drums together. At the same time his elbows smashed into the stomachs of the sailors who were holding him.

The oil drums rolled free on the heavily rolling deck. The sailors doubled over. And Indy was free to go for the man in the Panama hat.

The man tried to escape. But a rolling oil drum knocked him off his feet—and sent the Cross flying.

Indy was after it in a flash. He wound up skidding on his stomach along the wet deck to grab the Cross before it went overboard. Then he was on his feet to face a charging sailor.

Indy reached for the bullwhip on his belt. He

18

had come a long way since his first encounter with a lion tamer's whip. Now practice paid off. The bullwhip curled around the charging sailor's ankles and yanked him off his feet.

A blow from behind turned Indy around. Another sailor was there, his fist cocked to punch Indy out.

Instead, a rolling fuel drum put that second sailor out for the count, and Indy braced himself to take on the rest of the crew as they came for him.

Then he saw something that changed his mind—and made him hurdle over the railing into the raging sea.

He had seen an oil drum rolling toward a stack of crates. He was able to read the lettering on the crates: DANGER: TNT.

Indy hit the water just before the ship vanished in a giant explosion.

◆   ◆   ◆

"Funny thing, that ship was named *Vásquez de Coronado*," Indy said. "So I guess you could say that Coronado got his revenge on the thieves who stole his Cross."

"With a little help from you," said Marcus Brody.

Brody was curator of the archaeological museum at the college where Indiana Jones taught. He and Indy were in Brody's office, admiring Indy's latest contribution to the institution. The Cross of Coronado gleamed on Brody's desk.

"Lucky thing another ship came along," Indy recalled. "I don't know how long I could have managed to hang on to that life preserver I salvaged."

"Someday your luck is going to run out," Brody cautioned.

Indy shrugged. "No risk, no reward. And you have to admit, the Cross is quite a reward. Speaking of which, I've got a bill made up for my expenses. Hunting that Cross around the world didn't come cheap—not to mention the time I had to spend."

Brody coughed. "I'm sure we can work something out."

Indy looked at his watch. "I'll save the haggling for later. I have to make it to class. It's overbooked as usual. All those students waiting to learn about archaeology. All the nonsense about romance and adventure I have to get out of their heads."

Brody smiled. "And so many of them pretty girls. Strange how they flock to your classes. But it's a good thing you're such a popular teacher. Otherwise the college wouldn't be as lenient about letting you take so much time off."

"Yeah, those fuddy-duddies don't recognize the importance of fieldwork," said Indy.

"Especially when you go so far afield," said Brody.

"Well, I'll be happy to spend the rest of this term just teaching," said Indy. "In fact, now that I've recovered the Cross, maybe I'll give up globe-trotting for good. The Cross was always like a goad, driving me on."

"We'll see what the future holds," said Brody, smiling.

"Right now it holds a lecture about what hard, serious, often dull work archaeology is," said Indy, and left Brody's office to head to the classroom.

But four men in a long black car had other ideas.

The car pulled up to the curb as Indy walked across campus. One man got out and blocked Indy's path.

"Dr. Jones?" he said.

"Yes," said Indy.

"We'd like you to come with us," the man said.

"I'm afraid I have a class to go to," said Indy.

21

The man pulled back his jacket to reveal a pistol butt sticking out of a shoulder holster.

"And I'm afraid we have to insist."

◆　　　◆　　　◆

The car was fast. By early afternoon Indy was in New York City. Or rather he was *above* New York City, in the penthouse of a towering Fifth Avenue luxury building.

The men who brought him there left him alone in a large room. Indy's anger gave way to growing interest as he looked around him. The room was filled with old statues and other ancient artifacts from around the world.

"I hope you approve of my little collection," said a voice from the doorway.

Indy turned to see a tall, powerfully built man in dinner clothes enter. His hair was graying, but there was nothing middle-aged in the way he moved and spoke.

"Welcome, Dr. Jones," he said. "I'm Walter Donovan. Perhaps you've heard of me."

"Everyone in archaeology has heard of you," Indy said. "Your gifts to museums are famous. But I see you've kept some of your discoveries for yourself."

"A few pieces with sentimental value," said Donovan, dismissing the treasures in the room.

22

And for a man with his wealth, perhaps they were. "I have one piece, though, that is special. I'd like you to look at it."

"Is that why your goons shanghaied me?" asked Indy.

"Sorry about that," Donovan apologized. "But I think *this* will soothe your feelings."

Donovan showed Indy a stone tablet. Indy examined the inscriptions covering it.

"Early Christian symbols," he said. "Gothic characters. Byzantine carvings. Middle twelfth century. Where did you find it?"

"In the mountain regions north of Ankara," Donovan said. "Can you translate it?"

"Let's see. Some of it's pretty worn," said Indy, bending to the task. " 'He who drinks the water that I give him . . . will have a spring inside him welling up for eternal life. . . . Bring me to your holy mountain . . . across the desert . . . to the Canyon of the Crescent Moon, broad enough only for one man . . . to the Temple of the Sun, holy enough for all men . . .' "

Indy paused to make sure that he had read the next words right. Then he went on, " '. . . where the cup that holds the blood of Jesus Christ our Lord resides forever.' "

"The Holy Grail, Dr. Jones," Donovan said

softly. "The chalice used by Christ at the Last Supper. The cup that caught his blood at the Crucifixion. The lost relic that men have hunted for two thousand years."

"And have never found," said Indy, shrugging. "It's a bedtime story."

"The cup that gives eternal life to those who drink from it," Donovan went on, his eyes gleaming.

"An old man's dream," said Indy.

"Everyman's dream," said Donovan. "Including your father's."

"Grail lore is his obsession," said Indy with a grimace. He and his father disagreed on a lot of things, the Holy Grail among them.

"He's the foremost Grail scholar in the world," Donovan said.

"And he's welcome to be," Indy said. "He lives in a world of dusty old manuscripts. I prefer the real world beyond the library walls."

"Still, those old manuscripts tell interesting tales," Donovan persisted. "Like the story of the Grail being discovered by three knights of the First Crusade. Three knights who were also brothers."

"I've heard that bedtime story too," Indy said. "One hundred and fifty years after they found it, two of them walked out of the desert and began the long journey home. But only one made it. And before dying of *extreme* old age, he told his tale to a monk."

"And the monk in turn wrote it down," Donovan said, producing a brittle parchment manuscript. "This says that the knight declared that two 'markers' would reveal the location of the Grail. Dr. Jones, *this tablet is one of those markers.*"

"And the second marker?" Indy had to ask despite his doubts.

"The second marker is entombed with the knight's dead brother. The man heading the search I am financing is sure that tomb is in the city of Venice, Italy."

"And what about the third knight?" Indy asked. "Even a bedtime story should cover all the bases."

"The third knight stayed behind—to guard the Grail," Donovan said. He touched the manuscript with reverence. "It's all explained here. So you see, we're only one step away from completing the greatest quest in history."

"That last step is usually when the ground disappears from under your feet," was Indy's wry comment.

"You may be more right than you know," Donovan said.

"How so?" Indy asked.

"My man in charge of the search has vanished—along with all his research. We received a cable from his colleague, Dr. Schneider."

"Tough luck," said Indy.

"But good luck for you, Dr. Jones," said Donovan. "It gives you a crack at the greatest triumph an archaeologist could want. All you have to do is pick up my man's trail, find him—and you'll find the Grail."

"You've got the wrong Jones," said Indy. "You want the one who believes in this stuff. Try my father."

Donovan put his hand on Indy's shoulder. "I already have. He's the one who disappeared."

Chapter 3

THE NEXT DAY INDY PHONED DONOVAN WITH his answer.

"Okay, Donovan, I'll go to Venice," he said. "Get that plane you promised ready. And there'll be another passenger too. Marcus Brody."

"Brody? The museum curator?" Donovan was surprised. "I didn't know he was an adventurer like you."

"He's not," said Indy. "But he's my father's best and oldest friend. In fact, he's the one who convinced me to go. Whether or not I believe in the Grail, he made me see it was my duty to find my dad."

"Then I owe him my gratitude," Donovan

said. "Of course he's welcome to go. My Venice apartment is more than big enough for two. I'll wire Dr. Schneider, your father's assistant, to expect you both. And remember, when you get there, don't trust anyone."

"Believe me, I won't," Indy assured him.

Brody was with Indy when he made the call. As soon as Indy hung up, Brody asked, "You're sure you don't want to tell him about the diary?"

"I'm sure," Indy said. "Father sent that diary to me for a reason. Until we find out what it was, we should keep it to ourselves."

Indy had found the diary the night before. That was after he had gone to his father's house in Princeton with Marcus Brody. Perhaps with Brody's help, Indy might find a clue to Professor Henry Jones's whereabouts.

Instead they found the place ransacked, ripped apart from cellar to attic. What were the intruders hunting for? Indy was stumped—until he had a flash of memory. In his mind's eye he saw a thick envelope lying on his office desk, unopened like all the other mail that had piled up while he was away hunting the Cross. Its postmark made it stand out: Venice, Italy.

Brody stared wide-eyed at the speedometer as Indy drove back to campus. His eyes opened wider when Indy ripped open the envelope and pulled out a diary.

Brody recognized it at once. He had seen Henry Jones writing in it year after year, setting down all of his research on the Holy Grail. Brody told Indy that nothing short of the threat of death would have made Indy's father part with it.

Now Indy swore that nothing would make *him* part with it. Not until he had figured out the meaning of all the mysterious entries in it. Or until he could personally put it back into his father's hands.

◆   ◆   ◆

The diary was safe in Indy's leather jacket pocket when he and Brody arrived in Venice. Indy had spent the entire plane trip going through its closely written pages. But he had only succeeded in finding two pieces to start putting together the jigsaw puzzle. One was a pencil sketch of what seemed to be a stained-glass window. Below the sketch was a series of numbers. The other was a loose sheet of paper. On it was a rubbing of the tablet that Indy had viewed in Donovan's apartment.

"That rubbing means Dad was getting close to finding the second marker for the location of the so-called Holy Grail," said Indy as he and Marcus got off the water bus that had taken them to the Venice landing. Emerging in the dawning light of day were the beautiful ancient buildings of the city and the darkly rippling canals that served as its streets. "He wanted to put both markers together to see if they made sense."

"We can check with his assistant, Dr. Schneider," Marcus said. "Maybe he'll know for sure."

"Yeah, if we can find him," said Indy, looking around the crowded landing. "Where is the guy, anyway? He's supposed to be here to meet us."

At that moment Indy saw a couple of men in uniform grabbing a man dressed in shabby clothing. One of the uniformed thugs held the man from behind while the other started punching him. Indy tensed. But Marcus laid a restraining hand on his arm.

"Better not interfere," Marcus cautioned. "This isn't America. Mussolini is dictator here, and his police can do anything they want."

"Yeah, just like in Germany, under that crackpot Hitler," said Indy. With an effort he got a hold on himself. "I guess you're right, Marcus. I can't take on a whole country—though someday we Americans will have to."

"Right now we have our hands full just finding your father in this city we don't know at all," Marcus said. "I wish Dr. Schneider would show up. We need him."

"Well, maybe we can find another guide—like *her*, for instance," Indy said, his eyes lighting up.

He was looking at living proof that even if ugly things were happening in Italy, it still had some very attractive features—like the gorgeous young woman heading toward them.

Indy felt like he had hit a jackpot when she came right up to him and said, "Dr. Jones?"

"Yes," he said with an encouraging smile. Maybe she had seen his picture in the paper.

"I knew it was you," she said, with a warm smile of her own. "You have your father's eyes."

"And my mother's ears," said Indy. "The rest belongs to you."

But she had already turned to Marcus. "Marcus Brody?"

"That's right," said Marcus.

"Let me introduce myself," she said. "Elsa Schneider. *Dr.* Elsa Schneider."

◆   ◆   ◆

"So you were my father's assistant," Indy said. It was hours later, but Indy still was trying to get used to the idea of this knockout of a girl being a dedicated scholar.

There could be no doubt, though, that Elsa was one. She clearly knew her way around the old library where she had taken Indy and Marcus.

"This was the last place I saw your father," she said. "He was very close to tracking down the Knight's tomb. I had never seen him so excited. He was as giddy as a schoolboy."

"My father?" said Indy. "He was never giddy, even when he *was* a schoolboy."

"Maybe you didn't know your father very well— not as well as I," Elsa said.

Indy gave her a sharp look. Could she be hinting . . . ? No, impossible. "What I want to know now is what he found," Indy said in a businesslike voice.

"I have only one clue," Elsa said. "I left him sitting in this very room. He sent me out to find an ancient map of the city. When I returned, he was gone—and only this scrap of paper was left behind."

She handed it to Indy. He studied it. On it were the Roman numerals III, VII, and X.

"I've been trying to figure out those numbers all week," Elsa said. " 'Three, seven, ten.' I've read through every old book I could find. But no luck."

"A lot of work for nothing," Indy sympathized.

"It wasn't so bad," Elsa said. "I adore old books. A great library like this is like a temple to me."

"There is something holy about it," Marcus agreed.

"Actually, this library once was holy ground," Elsa said. "It used to be a Franciscan monastery. The columns in here were brought back from the sacking of Byzantium in the Crusades."

But Indy wasn't looking at the columns. He was looking at a stained-glass window depicting a knight. He whipped the diary out of his pocket and studied the sketch of the stained-glass window inside. This was it. And then he saw how the numbers fit in.

"See," he said as Marcus and Elsa looked over his shoulder. "The Roman numerals are worked into the design of the picture. Dad wasn't here to look for a book about the knight's tomb. He was looking for the tomb itself."

"I don't understand," said Elsa.

"I don't either," said Marcus.

"Check out this column," said Indy, his eyes moving as fast as his mind. "It's marked with a

III. We just have to find the VII and X and we're in business."

"Here's the VII—on this old bookshelf!" exclaimed Elsa.

"But the X—where is it?" Indy said impatiently.

The three of them hunted feverishly, but without success. "It has to be here," muttered Indy. He spotted a ladder leading to a balcony. He went up two rungs at a time. He looked around. Nothing. He shook his head in disgust and looked down. Then a big grin lit his face. "Bingo!"

On the floor of the library was an elaborate design in tile that formed a beautiful X.

"X marks the spot," said Indy as he and the others bent over it. He pried at the center tile with his Swiss army knife. For an agonizing moment, it held firm. Then it came up—to reveal a two-foot-square hole. From the hole came a blast of foul-smelling air.

Indy handed the diary to Marcus. "Keep this safe. I'm going down."

"Not before me," Elsa said. She already had lowered one leg into the hole.

"A girl with spirit," Indy said admiringly as he helped her descend. Then he followed her.

The only light below was from a cigarette

lighter that Elsa produced. The flame lit a tunnel of ancient stone. In niches in the walls were blackened human bones in rotting linen. On the walls were faded markings.

"Pagan symbols," said Elsa. "Fourth or fifth century."

"Right," said Indy. "About six hundred years before the Crusades."

"The Christians would have dug their own burial chambers farther on," said Elsa.

"That's where we'll find our knight," Indy said.

Five minutes later Indy and Elsa were deep into the tunnel and sloshing through green slimy water. They were also walking hand in hand. Indy wasn't sure when that had happened, but he *was* sure Elsa's hand felt pretty good. Elsa, in fact, was pretty good all around. She plowed ahead without flinching. Some girl.

"What's this?" Elsa wondered, indicating dark bubbles in the green slime.

"Oil," Indy said. "I could sink a well down here and retire."

"Look," Elsa said. "Hebrew markings on the wall. We're getting closer to the Christian era."

"Yeah, here's a picture of the Ark of the Covenant," said Indy. "The Lost Ark."

"Are you sure?" Elsa asked.

"Pretty sure," said Indy, deadpan. Then he said, "There's a passageway up ahead. Maybe that's it."

Elsa peered into it first. *"Ughh,"* she said.

Indy gave a look and said, *"Rats."*

It was an understatement. It was a scene straight out of a nightmare. Rats upon rats upon rats. Thousands, maybe millions—squealing, squirming, thrashing in the shallow water, and already dashing between Elsa's and Indy's legs, trying to nip at their ankles.

"There's a ledge we can walk on—if you're game," Indy said.

Elsa didn't bother answering. She simply started edging down the thin passageway on the narrow outcropping of stone above the living sea of rats.

"Got to hand it to Dad. He sure knew how to pick an assistant," Indy said to himself as he followed her.

"This must be it," Elsa said with excitement when they reached the entrance to a large chamber.

The water was deeper here, except at the center of the room. There, a stone platform rose like an island. On the platform were massive coffins.

"I'll go first," Indy said. "This may be tricky."

He moved ahead of Elsa, took a step into the room, and plunged up to his chest in black, oily water. He grinned. "See what I mean?"

Keeping their chins high, they were able to make it to the platform. Dripping, they climbed onto it.

"Beautiful work," said Indy, inspecting the coffins. "True medieval artistry."

"This is the one we want," Elsa said. "It's by far the finest. Look at the carvings and the scrollwork."

Indy nodded. Elsa knew her stuff. She was loyal, too. Her first words when they pushed the coffin lid off were, "The Knight! If only your father were here to see it."

Indy, though, was less interested in the bones of a knight in full armor than in the engraving on his shield.

It was the same style as the one on the tablet in Donovan's apartment. The shield was the second marker!

Quickly he took the paper with the rubbing of Donovan's tablet from his pocket. He laid it over the shield. The partial message of the tablet was now complete. Eagerly Indy began to make a rubbing from the shield to put the two fragments permanently together.

"Where did that come from?" Elsa asked.

"Trade secret," said Indy, working away.

"This is no time for professional rivalry—not with your father in such danger," Elsa said.

But that was as far as the argument got.

"Hold it!" Indy commanded, jerking his head up and jamming the completed rubbing into his leather jacket pocket.

What he heard was a distant roaring, followed by a chattering, squeaking, squealing sound. Then he saw a glow lighting the chamber entrance, only to be blotted out by a vast horde of terrified, fleeing rats.

"Fire!" he shouted above the din. "The oil's on fire!"

Elsa screamed as rats washed over them and a giant fireball filled the chamber entrance.

With both hands Indy shoved the Knight's coffin off the platform so that it fell upside down into the water. Then he grabbed Elsa and threw her in.

"Get under the coffin! Air pocket!" he shouted, and dove in himself.

A moment later they were both neck deep in water, under the cover of the coffin. But they were not alone. With them was the Knight, his skull grinning at them.

"Sorry, pal, three's a crowd," said Indy, and

shoved the remains down and out of their refuge.

But at the same time more company was arriving. Rats were frantically gnawing through the wood and dropping, with fur aflame, into the water around them.

Then smoke began to fill the air.

"The coffin's on fire!" Elsa screamed.

"At least that takes care of the rats," said Indy. "Tell me, can you swim?"

"Austrian Swim Team," Elsa said. "1932 Olympics. Silver medal in the fifty-meter freestyle."

"A simple yes or no!" said Indy. "Take a deep breath. We'll have to swim under the fire."

Elsa was already extending her arms for the plunge.

"Want to have a race?" she asked. "Just to make it interesting?"

Chapter 4

"GOOD THING THERE WAS AN AIR SHAFT LEADING out of that burial chamber," said Indy. "Otherwise we'd be history—just like the Knight down there."

"I'd much rather be surrounded by history—especially when it's as beautiful as this," Elsa said.

The two of them stood in dripping clothes on the bank of the lagoon that served as Venice's harbor. As the sun dried them they gazed at the broad expanse of St. Mark's Square, where a great cathedral reigned in eternal splendor over the crowds of tourists and pigeons.

Suddenly Indy stiffened.

"Trouble is—there's no getting away from the present," he said. "Come on. We'll make a run for it."

A commanding man with an imposing mustache and two followers were heading toward them. All had guns. When Indy and Elsa started running, the men gave chase.

"What—?" Elsa gasped as she ran beside Indy.

"No time for questions," said Indy. "Just action."

At that moment he spied a moored speedboat. Without breaking stride he jumped into it. Elsa followed. Indy cast off the line, started the engine—but not quickly enough.

One of the gunmen, faster than the others, leaped over the widening strip of water and into the boat.

He didn't stay aboard for long. Indy's chop to the wrist sent the gun flying from his hand. Then a right to the stomach and a left to the jaw sent him over the side.

Rubbing his knuckles, Indy picked up the gun. Only then did he notice that Elsa was behind the wheel of the boat and handling it with evident expertise.

Indy grinned. "Should have known you'd be

good at this, too. But now we'll have to see how good."

Two speedboats were coming after them. The man with the mustache was in one, with a follower in the other. To make things worse, Indy saw a gigantic steamer looming in front of them, heading for shore. And Elsa was heading their boat for the narrowing strip of water between the steamer and the dock.

"Are you crazy?" Indy tried to shout over the din of the engine. "Don't go between them!"

Elsa didn't quite get the message.

"I should go between them?" she shouted back. "Are you crazy?"

But still she tried to do what she thought Indy wanted. Indy had no time to wrench the wheel from her hands as the boat shot into the closing space between the huge ship and the massive wharf. He could only shut his eyes.

Second later, he opened them to see clear water all around.

"Great work, baby," he said. "We made it."

"Our friend didn't," said Elsa, gesturing backward with her head while keeping her hands on the wheel.

Indy looked back. One speedboat had been turned to splinters when it tried to follow them through the closing gap.

"That'll teach them to fool with a team like us," said Indy. But his smile faded when he heard a different noise from that of the engine—an unmistakable chatter.

Indy turned to see the other speedboat closing in on him. The mustached man was at the wheel, flanked by a henchman holding a blazing machine gun.

"We'll have to outrace them!" Indy shouted to Elsa as he fired off a futile pistol shot while machine-gun slugs chewed at the wood hull of their boat.

Suddenly their engine died, killed by bullets.

Their boat was drifting helplessly, right into the giant propellers of a huge ocean liner dead ahead.

Meanwhile the enemy speedboat was pulling up alongside them.

"Time to go to Plan B," Indy said, and led Elsa in leaping onto the enemy boat while their own boat was sucked to destruction.

The startled machine gunner was knocked backward, his weapon sent flying, by Indy's unexpected charge.

"Swim for it, champion!" Indy shouted to Elsa as he grappled with his opponent and plunged overboard with him.

As he fell he heard Elsa's horrified scream.

She had to think he was a goner, raw meat for the liner's propellers. He hoped she would keep her cool enough to use the confusion to swim for shore.

Right now, though, Indy had himself to worry about. He seized the gunwale of the boat with both hands and kicked out at his opponent with both feet. He felt a solid thump. He didn't have to worry about *that* guy anymore.

Hauling himself back onto the boat, Indy saw that Elsa had seized her chance to escape. Meanwhile the man with the mustache, his back toward Indy, was turning the boat around to escape the liner's propellers.

Smiling grimly, Indy snapped off the speedboat's engine. Then he went for the man with the mustache, pinning him against the wheel.

"All right, now talk," he commanded fiercely. *"Where is my father?"*

It was then that things really started going wrong.

First, the speedboat drifted into the liner's propellers, which commenced to chew the craft up, from the back toward the front, where Indy held his captive.

And second, the man with the mustache wasn't scared.

44

"You foolish man," he said calmly. "What are you doing? If you don't let me go, we'll both die."

"Then we'll die!" shouted Indy, wild with rage.

Then he saw something that took away his rage and replaced it with a question mark.

In pinning the man, he had ripped open the man's shirt. On his chest was a tattoo. It was in the shape of a Christian cross—but a cross whose longer end tapered to form the point of a sword.

"Maybe we'd better talk," said Indy.

"It's too late for that, Dr. Jones," the man with the mustache shouted above the crunching of the propellers that were chewing away at the boat. "Prepare to meet your Maker—as I am prepared to meet mine."

Then there was another sound—of a speed-boat engine. And another voice—Elsa's.

"See what I found on my swim!" she shouted from behind the wheel of a gleaming new speed-boat. "Hop aboard!"

◆   ◆   ◆

"My name is Kazim," said the man with the mustache, pouring small glasses of tea for Indy and Elsa. They were in his hotel room, where

45

he had taken them after they docked. "My fore-
bears were princes of an empire that stretched
from Morocco to the Caspian Sea."

"Allah be praised," Indy said politely.

Kazim wrinkled his nose in contempt. "*I*
am talking about the Christian empire of
Byzantium."

"Right," said Indy. "And a great empire it
was. But if you don't mind my asking, what has
this to do with your trying to kill me?"

"And me," said Elsa.

"And her," Indy added. "She's with me."

"The Grail has been safe for a thousand years,"
Kazim said. "And for all that time, the Brotherhood of the Cruciform Sword has been there to
protect it."

"The Brotherhood of the Cruciform Sword?"
said Indy, staring at the tattoo on Kazim's chest.

Kazim nodded. "I am in charge of guarding
the first place where those who seek the Grail
would look. I watched your search every step of
the way."

"And my father?" said Indy, his hands clench-
ing into fists. "Did you watch him, too? Did you
want to stop him as well?"

"We were deciding what to do about him
when others saved us the trouble by taking him
away," said Kazim.

"What others?" asked Indy, leaning forward.

"Before I answer," said Kazim, "tell me if you seek the Cup of Christ for His glory or for yours?"

"I didn't come for the Cup of Christ," Indy said. "I came to find my father. And as for him, it is not personal reward he seeks, but eternal truth for all mankind."

Kazim looked deeply into Indy's eyes for a long moment. Then he said, "I have been trained to see if men tell the truth or lie. I see that I can believe you. Your father is being held in Brunwald Castle on the Austrian-German border."

"Brunwald," Elsa said. "It's near where I grew up." She turned to Indy. "I'll be your guide, if you want me."

Indy didn't have to say a word. His eyes said it all. He definitely wanted her around.

◆　　　◆　　　◆

Before they left, though, Indy wanted one more thing. He wanted to see Marcus Brody. Alone.

He found Marcus in the apartment Donovan had provided for them.

"Where's Dr. Schneider?" Marcus asked.

"I sent Elsa off to pack her things," said Indy. "I didn't want her around while we try to figure out the meaning of the rubbing I made of the Knight's shield."

"Don't you trust her?" Marcus asked, raising his eyebrows.

"It's not that," Indy said. "I'd trust her with my life. In fact, she's already saved it once. But we're going into dangerous territory—and the less she knows, the less she's liable to get hurt if things go wrong."

Indy told Marcus about Brunwald Castle. Then they got down to the business of deciphering the rubbing.

Fortunately, though the paper was damp, the leather of Indy's jacket had kept the rubbing from being ruined. Brody, with his trained museum curator's eyes, was the first to spot the name it revealed.

"Alexandretta," Marcus said excitedly.

Indy was excited too. The name rang a bell.

"The Knights of the First Crusade laid siege to Alexandretta for over a year," he said. "The entire city was destroyed." Indy went to a world atlas and opened it to a map of the Middle East. His finger jabbed down on the principality of Hatay, on the border of Syria. "*Here* is where Alexandretta once was. The present city of Iskenderun is built on its ruins. And look, this is the desert and mountains that the Grail Tablet described. Somewhere in these mountains must be the Canyon of the Crescent Moon. But where?"

"Your father would know," Marcus said. "In fact, he *did* know."

"What do you mean?" asked Indy.

"Look at this map he drew in his diary," Marcus said. "He must have pieced it together from hundreds of sources over the last forty years. It maps out a course due east from the city, across the desert to an oasis. Then it stretches south to a river which leads to a mountain range, and on into the canyon. But he didn't know *what* city or *which* desert."

"But *we* know," said Indy, his eyes glowing. He slapped his fist into his palm. "Marcus, get to Iskenderun. I'll wire Sallah in Cairo to join you. He's the best digger in the business. Between you, you can get an expedition organized fast. I want everything ready to go when Elsa and I join you there—*with Dad.*"

Chapter 5

THUNDER RUMBLED OVER THE AUSTRIAN ALPS as Indy and Elsa stood staring at the forbidding stone walls of Brunwald Castle. Indy checked to make sure his bullwhip was securely attached to his belt.

"What are you going to do with that?" asked Elsa.

"Whatever I have to," said Indy. "You'd be surprised how it comes in handy."

He felt a raindrop splatter on his nose and headed for the massive oaken front door.

"Let's get in where it's safe and dry." He grinned and added, "Dry, at least."

"How do we get in?" Elsa asked.

"I don't know," Indy said. "I'll think of something."

"Perhaps this will help inspire you," Elsa said. She put both arms around his neck and kissed him.

Indy returned the kiss. And when they both came up for air he said, "Hey, we're getting pretty good at this."

It was the latest in a string of kisses that had extended from Venice to Austria. Elsa had turned out to be not only a dedicated scholar, a crack swimmer, and a cool-headed partner in hot spots, but a warm-blooded woman as well. She was the kind of companion, in fact, that Indy had been looking for his whole life. His father might have had a good eye in choosing Elsa as an assistant. But Indy was figuring on going his old man one better.

"Now, back to business," Indy said, knocking loudly on the door. "Wish me luck."

"I'm sure you won't need it," said Elsa, smiling affectionately.

A tall man in butler's clothing opened the door.

"Yes?" he said, looking down his long nose at Indy and Elsa as they stood in what was now a downpour.

"About time!" said Indy indignantly, in his best upper-class British accent. "We're drenched!"

Without hesitating, he pushed his way past the butler, dragging Elsa with him.

"Are you expected?" the butler sputtered.

"Don't take that tone with *me*," Indy said. "Buttle off and tell your master that Lord Clarence Chumley and his assistant are here to view the tapestries."

"Tapestries?" said the butler.

"My good man, this *is* a castle, isn't it?" Indy demanded. "It *must* have tapestries."

"This is a castle," said the butler. "We have tapestries. And if you're an English lord, I'm Jesse Owens."

The butler didn't get a chance to laugh at his own joke. Indy's fist connected with his chin. He went down like a felled tree.

Indy shook his head. "One simply can't *find* good servants anymore," he commented. Then he said in his normal voice, "Come on, let's find Dad."

"Where could he be?" wondered Elsa.

"Maybe in the dungeons," said Indy. "But no, that would be too corny."

Suddenly, without warning, he grabbed Elsa's

arm and pulled her with him behind a statue of a Brunwald ancestor. A pair of chatting soldiers came out of a room down the hall and went up the wide, curving stairway. They wore black uniforms, death's head insignia, and swastika armbands.

"Nazi SS," Indy whispered. "Trained killers."

When the coast was clear, Indy and Elsa started their search of the castle, ducking behind pillars when more soldiers appeared and dashing past open doors of rooms filled with German voices.

Reaching the top floor, they edged along a deserted corridor. It came to a dead end at a locked door.

"This one," said Indy. "I bet he's in here." He pointed to an electrical connection. "It's the only room on this floor that's wired." He tapped the door. "Too thick to break through. Have to find a way around it. Come on."

With Elsa close behind, Indy tried a door down the corridor. It swung open. He entered and headed straight for the floor-to-ceiling window, with Elsa half running to keep up with him. He opened the window wide and peered out through slanting rain lit by lightning

53

flashes. He nodded to himself and took out his bullwhip.

"Wait here," he told Elsa, and climbed up onto the window ledge.

"But you can't—" Elsa began.

"Don't worry," Indy assured her. "Child's play."

Like a fly fisherman he cast out the lash of his whip. Its end curled around a gargoyle on the castle roof. Indy tugged to make sure it was secure, then swung out on it, through the driving rain, and over the ground far below.

He landed on a narrow window ledge and let out his breath. Then he sucked in more air and swung to another ledge. And another. And another—until he stood on the window ledge of the locked room.

"Shoot," he said. A locked wooden shutter covered the window.

He saw a flashlight shining from the castle roof and heard the barking of Dobermans. A patrol! Pressing against the shutters, he barely escaped the light beam.

"No time to play around," Indy muttered. Gripping the whip handle tightly, he pushed off from the window ledge as hard as he could. He turned himself into a human pendulum, coming back toward the shuttered window with his feet extended like battering rams.

It worked. He went crashing through the shutters and landed in the dimly lit room. Grinning, Indy turned to haul his whiplash in—and never saw what hit him as he felt the smashing blow on the back of his head, heard the shattering noise, and saw the lights go out.

◆　　　◆　　　◆

The next thing he knew, a familiar voice was saying, "Junior!"

He opened his eyes and said to his father, "Don't call me that!"

Professor Henry Jones, as usual, paid no attention to his son's wishes. "Junior, what are you doing here?"

"What do you think?" said Indy. "I've come to save you. You gave me quite a welcome."

"I'll never forgive myself," said Henry.

"Oh, we all make mistakes," Indy said generously.

Then he saw that his father was looking at the vase he had broken over Indy's head.

"Late fourteenth century, Ming Dynasty," said Henry sadly. Then he examined its broken handle and brightened. "Thank goodness! It's a fake."

Indy was looking too. "Right. You can tell by the cross section."

Henry tossed away the handle and said, "By the way, sorry about your head. I thought you were one of *them*."

"*They* can come in through the door," Indy said.

"Good point," Henry said. "I was wrong. But I was certainly right to mail you the diary. Did you get it?"

"I got it and used it," said Indy.

"You found the entrance to the catacombs? The Knight? The shield? The inscription? The location?" Henry's voice trembled with excitement.

"Alexandretta," Indy said.

"Of *course,* I should have guessed," said Henry. "On the pilgrim trail from the Eastern Empire." He put his hand on Indy's shoulder. "Good work, Junior."

Indy winced, but said nothing. Compliments from his father were too rare to argue with. He could only respond, "It was your work too. Your diary."

"Thank God the Nazis didn't get their hands on it when they grabbed me," said Henry with satisfaction. "I could take their torture, knowing it was safe far away from here."

Indy cleared his throat. "Yeah. Right. Well, let's get out of here—fast."

"Too late," said his father as the door of the room was kicked open.

Three SS men entered. Two held submachine guns. The third was an officer with a big smile on his face.

"Dr. Jones," he said, "I'll take the book now."

He was talking to Indy. But it was Henry who answered, "You dolt! You really think my son would be stupid enough to bring the diary all the way back to the very place where—" Then he stopped as a thought hit him. "You didn't, did you, Junior?"

"Uh, well, the thing is—" Indy babbled.

Henry put his hand over his eyes. "I should have mailed it to the Marx Brothers. How *could* you, Junior?"

"Don't call me Junior," Indy roared, grabbing a submachine gun out of the hands of a startled soldier, and spraying all three Nazis with it.

Henry stared at the riddled bodies. "I don't believe what you just did, Junior."

"Sometimes *I* don't believe what I do, either,"

Indy said. "Now let's make tracks. We've one more stop to make in the castle, then we're out of here."

"Stop? What stop?" asked Henry.

"You'll see," Indy said. His dad's eyes would pop when he saw his devoted assistant was in on the rescue. It would really make the old man's day.

But when they entered the room where Elsa was waiting, all Henry could say was, "Oh, no!"

◆   ◆   ◆

Elsa wasn't alone. With her was an SS colonel. He had one arm around her waist. With his other arm he held a Luger pistol to her head.

"That's far enough, Dr. Jones," the Nazi said. "Throw down your weapon."

"Don't do it, Junior," Henry said. "She's with them."

"Put down the gun or the girl dies," the Nazi cut in.

"Please, do it!" Elsa pleaded.

"Don't!" Henry commanded.

"Enough! She dies!" the Nazi snarled, jamming the Luger barrel into Elsa's neck.

She screamed in pain.

Something inside Indy snapped.

"Wait!" he said, and threw his submachine gun to the floor.

"*Junior*," Henry groaned as the Nazi let Elsa go.

She ran forward and threw herself into Indy's arms.

"Sorry . . . I'm so sorry . . ." she sobbed, her lips close to his ear. "But you should have listened to your father," she concluded, as her hand snaked the diary out of Indy's pocket and she stepped away from him.

"You mean you're a . . ." Indy gasped.

A voice from the doorway answered the question.

"Yes, Dr. Schneider is a loyal servant of the Third Reich, as am I. Good work, Elsa. And you too, Colonel Vogel. But I am disappointed in you, Indiana Jones. I *told* you to trust no one."

"Oh, *no*," said Indy as he turned to see the imposing, elegantly clothed figure of Walter Donovan. For a second his vision glazed over. He felt like a fighter slugged by a one-two punch.

Meanwhile his father grimaced in disgust. "Donovan. I knew you would sell your own mother for an Etruscan vase. But I didn't know

59

you'd sell your country and your soul to this bunch of madmen."

Then he turned to Indy. "If only you had listened to me, Junior."

"But how did you know Elsa was one of them?" Indy asked.

"One day, in her room, I spotted a suspicious letter—a letter from Berlin," said Henry.

"In her room?" said Indy, feeling more and more punch-drunk. "What were you doing in her room?"

Henry cleared his throat uncomfortably.

"You mean that you and she . . . she and you . . . ?" Indy said.

"Dr. Schneider is a most attractive woman, as you may have noticed," Henry said.

"I noticed," agreed Indy as his eyes met his father's, and both men shook their heads in regret.

Their heads snapped around as Donovan bellowed, "The map! Where's the map?"

He was looking in the diary. Elsa was next to him.

"The book had a map," she explained to Vogel. "A map with precise directions from an unknown city to the secret canyon of the Grail.

Indy and Herman break away from their Boy Scout troop and do a little exploring of their own.

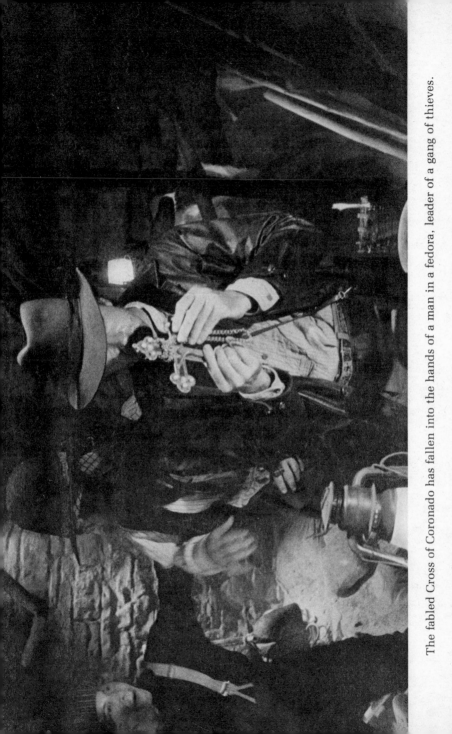

The fabled Cross of Coronado has fallen into the hands of a man in a fedora, leader of a gang of thieves.

When Indy captures the Cross, the thieves chase him onto a circus train.

Indy grabs the Cross, but he's got to defend himself against a charging lion. Luckily, there's a bullwhip close at hand.

Indy flees over a catwalk. Below him is a vat of squirming snakes!

Indy's university class in archaeology is always overbooked.

Donovan, a multimillionaire collector, tells Indy of his search for the Holy Grail.

Elsa, the beautiful Austrian archaeologist, joins Indy on a tour of a rat-infested underground burial chamber.

SS Colonel Vogel threatens to kill Elsa unless Indy throws down his gun.

Their boat riddled with bullets, Indy and Elsa dock with the help of Kazim, who explains his own mission in Venice.

As flames engulf them, Indy and his father, Henry, struggle to free themselves.

An historic meeting—Indiana Jones and Adolf Hitler.

Indy collects tickets aboard a German zeppelin.

Vogel and Indy struggle on top of a German tank
not far from the Temple of the Holy Grail.

Henry, dying of gunshot wounds,
urges Indy to find the Grail.

Indy, Henry, Sallah, and Marcus Brody ride through a canyon toward the Temple of the Grail.

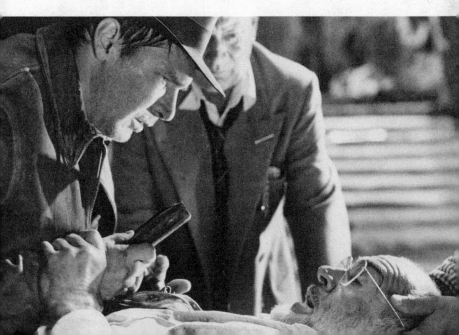

Indy helps the mysterious Grail Knight to his feet.

Confronted with many grails, Elsa and Indy try to make the right choice.

In trying to save Elsa, Indy is pulled over the edge of the abyss.
Only his father can save him.

Chapter 6

"I MUST GO TO BERLIN," ELSA TOLD INDY AND Henry. "I am making a speech at the Institute of Aryan Culture. Hitler himself will be there. I'll be able to show him the diary as proof of progress. It will guarantee continued support for this project."

"Congratulations," said Henry bitterly. "Your 'scholarship' is bearing golden fruit."

"You can tell us all about it when you get back, since it doesn't look like we're going anywhere," said Indy. He and his father were tied up tightly in back-to-back chairs. "That is, if we're still breathing."

"Don't worry, you won't be harmed," Elsa said. "Isn't that so, Herr Donovan?"

"Of course, my dear," Donovan assured her. "We may have to play rough sometimes in this hard world. But we're not savages. Besides, we may need these two if we don't find Brody. Isn't that right, Vogel?"

"Of course," said Vogel. "I am a German soldier. We do not murder helpless captives."

"You see, the people I work with are not so bad," Elsa said. She went to Indy, bent down, and kissed him warmly on the lips. "This is how we Austrians say good-bye."

With a regretful glance backward, she left the room.

Smiling thinly, Vogel strode over to Indy. He cocked his right hand and delivered a smashing punch to Indy's jaw. "And this is how we Germans say good-bye."

Chuckling, he left the room with Donovan.

Indy shook his head to clear it. "I like the Austrian way better," he muttered. Then he said to his father, "Did you see that wink Donovan gave Vogel when Elsa promised they wouldn't kill us? We have to get out of here fast—before they find Marcus."

"Nonsense," Henry said. "We have time to

think things through, come up with a foolproof plan. You said yourself that Brody would blend in. Disappear."

"You kidding?" Indy said. "I made all that up. Donovan said Marcus would be lost outside a museum. Well, I once saw Marcus get lost in *his* museum."

After a sweaty struggle with the ropes Henry said, "I give up. The knots are too good. German efficiency."

Indy had no better luck. But he was able to squirm around in his chair so that he half faced his father.

"Can you get a hand into my jacket pocket?" Indy said.

Henry grunted. "Yes, barely. But what—?" Then he felt something and pulled it out. "A cigarette lighter. But why—?" Then it hit him. "Junior, you're a pip!"

The lighter flame leaped up, licking against the rope on Henry's wrist and then against the wrist itself.

"Owwww!" Henry howled, and the lighter dropped onto a carpet that looked as old as the castle itself.

Within moments the bone-dry fabric was in flames.

"Well, let's try Plan B," said Indy, starting to rock his chair. "We head for the fireplace over there. It's the only thing in the room that won't burn."

Desperately using their bodies to propel their chairs, they made it to the huge fireplace.

"Well, Junior?" Henry asked. "Got a Plan C?"

At that moment Indy's foot came down on a flagstone. It gave way like a pedal being pushed. And the entire fireplace, flagstone floor included, began to silently rotate away from the burning room.

But what met their eyes in the room they rotated into were the backs of four SS radiomen bent over their equipment.

"Out of the fire, into the frying pan," Henry said as one of the Nazis turned and drew his pistol.

"Plan D," said Indy, spotting a lever near his head. He butted it with his skull as a bullet whizzed by his ear. The fireplace rotated them out of the radio room as other shots missed the moving mark.

A wall of flame faced them on the other side.

"We were better off back there!" Henry groaned.

"Plan E," Indy said. He had found a rough

stone in the fireplace to use to saw away his ropes. As soon as he was free, he untied his father. "Now we—"

Just then the fireplace began rotating again. There was no place to go in the burning room. They had to stay on this not-so-merry-go-round.

"On the other side, we jump the Nazis fast," Indy said.

"Faster than their bullets?" Henry asked wryly.

"You've got a point there," Indy acknowledged.

But the radio room was empty.

"All the Nazis must have gone after us," Indy said. He broke off a chair leg and jammed it in the rotator mechanism. "They won't be coming back. Let's get moving."

"Not so fast, Junior," Henry said. "Enough mad dashing about. Time to sit down and think out our next move."

"Sit down?" said Indy. "Are you crazy?"

"Stop panicking," said Henry as he eased himself down on a big overstuffed sofa. "I often find if I sit calmly"—the sofa gave a click, and the floor opened to reveal a staircase—"a solution presents itself."

"Plan F," said Indy, and they headed down the stairs. At the bottom, they stopped and stared.

"Got to hand it to those Nazis, they do things in a big way," said Indy, shaking his head in wonder.

In a cavern below the castle a huge secret military supply center had been built to take advantage of an underground river. Moored to steel piers were cargo ships, gunboats, and motorboats.

"Plan G," said Indy, pointing to a gleaming speedboat. But as he and his father jumped into it, he spotted Vogel running toward the piers at the head of a detachment of soldiers. Indy gunned the motor—then grabbed his dad and jumped for shore as the empty boat shot off.

"What are we doing, if I may ask?" Henry said.

"Plan H," said Indy. "Vogel will be chasing that boat—while we jump on that motorcycle over there."

Outside the castle, as the cycle roared along a deserted road with Indy driving and his father in the sidecar, Henry asked, "Would you say this has been just another typical day for you?"

"No," Indy said, "it's been better than most." He grinned and skidded the cycle to a stop. They were at a crossroads signpost. One arrow pointed south to Budapest. The other pointed north to Berlin.

"Off to Budapest," said Indy, turning the front wheel.

But his father grabbed his wrist.

"We go to Berlin," Henry said. "For my diary."

"Why? Brody has the map," said Indy.

"You didn't tear out enough pages," Henry said. "He who finds the Grail must face devices of lethal cunning. I managed to find the ways to get past those booby traps."

"Well, can't you *remember* them?" Indy demanded.

"I wrote them down so I didn't *have* to remember," Henry said.

"Half the German army is after us by now," Indy said. "Marcus is in danger. And you want to abandon him, and risk our lives by going right into the lion's den? All for that Grail of yours?" He grimaced. "You scholars. All you care about is pride and plunder."

That was as far as he got. His father slapped him hard across the face.

"That's for blasphemy. The quest for the Cup is not archaeology; it's a race against evil. If the Nazis get the Grail, they will rule the earth."

"I never understood your obsession with the Grail," said Indy. "And Mother didn't either."

"She did—too well," said Henry. "She kept her illness from me until all I could do was mourn her."

Indy rubbed his cheek. "Let's get to Berlin, Pop."

◆   ◆   ◆

"Ah, Berlin," Indy said. "The scent of linden trees—and the odor of burning books."

It was evening in the Nazi capital. The darkness was lit by a huge bonfire into which brownshirted young men with swastika armbands were hurling book after book. This orgy of destruction of the wisdom and beauty of the ages had begun when Hitler came to power, and showed no signs of ending.

Henry winced at the sight. "I pray that someday Germany awakes from this nightmare."

"I just hope that the rest of the world wakes up to what's happening here," said Indy. Then he said, "How do I look? I wish that Nazi officer was closer to my size. His uniform fits me like a tent."

"You can always say you're losing weight for the Fatherland," Henry said.

Suddenly Indy's arm shot out. *"Heil Hitler!"*

he yelled as he crossed the fingers of his other hand.

Passing before them was the Nazi leader himself, his eyes aglow with what some called genius and others called madness. Around him were high officials and armed guards. And walking beside him was Elsa. Indy felt sick as he saw Hitler pat her approvingly on the shoulder.

"Guess she got what she wanted," Indy muttered. He saw Elsa leaving Hitler's group and he told his father, "Wait here. Now I get what *I* want."

Elsa didn't notice him until he grabbed her by the arm and pulled her into an alleyway.

"Indy!" she gasped. Her face lit up with joy.

"Where is it?" he asked grimly. He didn't wait for her answer. Frisking her, he found what he was looking for.

"You came here for the *book*? But why?" Elsa asked.

"I didn't want to see it burned up by your friends," said Indy.

"I'm not one of them," Elsa protested. "I believe in the Grail. Not the Nazi swastika."

"Who cares what you believe?" said Indy. "I care about what you've done."

"You can't take the diary," Elsa said. "I only have to scream."

Indy's hands went around her neck. "I only have to squeeze."

"You'd never do it," Elsa said, looking him in the eyes.

"Neither would you," Indy said, returning her gaze and letting his hands drop.

Silently Elsa stood and sadly watched Indy turn his back on her and walk away.

"You got it?" Henry asked as soon as he saw Indy.

"I got it," said Indy, patting his pocket.

"I hope you didn't have to hurt Elsa," Henry said.

"No, at least not the way you mean," Indy said.

At that moment Indy and his father were caught up in a jostling crowd of children. Going with the flow, Indy saw what they wanted. Hitler had paused to hand out autographs.

Then Indy saw one of Hitler's elite guards staring curiously at him. Immediately Indy thrust the diary toward the scribbling Nazi leader. Hitler grabbed it, flipped it open, and scrawled his name.

As he handed the diary back to Indy, their eyes met. Indy shivered at what he saw.

The guy is like a hypnotist—a madman who can make a whole country nuts, Indy thought as he watched Hitler and his entourage move away through the cheering mob.

Suddenly a hand dropped on Indy's shoulder. He whirled to face the SS guard who had spotted him.

"Your papers," the man demanded.

"Heil Hitler!" Indy said at the top of his lungs. His arm shot out again—but this time his hand turned into a fist that took the guard out for the count.

No one noticed the KO. All eyes were fixed on Hitler as he climbed into his open-topped Mercedes.

"Time to go," Indy told his father. "I think we've outworn our welcome."

"How do we get out of fortress Germany?" Henry asked. "Plan Z?"

"I'm clean out of plans," Indy said. "From here on in we wing it."

Chapter 7

"IF WE CAN'T WING IT, THIS IS THE NEXT BEST thing," said Indy. He and his father were aboard a giant zeppelin, a gleaming, metal-sheathed, lighter-than-air craft ten stories tall and longer than two football fields. The Nazi secret police, the Gestapo, had been checking out everyone boarding all regular plane flights. But no one had interfered with those privileged enough to travel on the pride of the German air fleet.

As Indy and Henry waited for the moorings to be cast off, they sipped champagne and studied the diary.

" 'The challenges will number three,' " Henry read. " 'First, the Breath of God, only the penitent man will pass. Second, the Word of God, only in the footsteps of God will he proceed. Third, the Path of God, only in the leap from the lion's head will he prove his worth.' "

"Meaning what?" Indy asked.

"We'll find that out when we get there," Henry said.

"*If* we get there," said Indy. "Don't look now, but our pal Vogel has arrived. How that guy gets around!"

Vogel stood at the cabin entrance, scanning faces.

"Hide your face behind a magazine while I see what I can do," said Indy.

Keeping his back to Vogel, Indy, in his over-sized Nazi uniform, went down the aisle and through a door at the cabin rear. A minute later he reappeared, wearing a very undersized white flight attendant's jacket.

"Tickets. Ticket, please," he called out as he headed for Vogel. Vogel didn't look at his face until Indy had grabbed him by the collar.

Before Vogel could say a word, and as the zeppelin trembled and began to rise, Indy flung open the door and tossed Vogel out onto the runway.

Indy turned to face the horrified passengers.

"No ticket," he explained.

After collecting all the tickets desperately thrust at him, Indy went to the rear for another quick change. When he returned, Berlin was already far, far below.

"Bye-bye, Third Reich," Indy said.

"But won't the Nazis radio the crew to turn back?" asked Henry.

"Nobody is going to hear them," said Indy. "Not after the job I did on the radio. Wonder what's for dinner. I've worked up quite an appetite—and we've got a long flight ahead."

But they had barely finished after-dinner coffee and brandy when Indy said, "Maybe this flight is going to be shorter than I thought."

"Delicious," said Henry, wiping his mouth with a fine linen napkin. Then he said, "What do you mean?"

"Feel the zeppelin," said Indy. "We're turning around, going back to Germany."

At that moment a voice boomed over a loudspeaker. "Attention everyone! There are spies aboard the airship! Everyone loyal to the *Führer* join in the search!"

The passengers, however, remained seated. The brandy was simply too good to be gulped, especially since they could have as much as they wanted, and all of them had.

"Come on, Dad," said Indy. *"Heil Hitler!"* he shouted as he and his father headed for the rear.

There Indy saw a radioman listening intently to what was coming in over his earphones. The man never heard what hit him.

Indy looked at the repairs made on the radio. "They must have had a bunch of spare parts," he muttered. "More German efficiency. They have a knack of thinking of everything." Then he grinned. "Hey, I just thought of something myself. Let's go!"

"Go where?" Henry asked.

"They've got a tiny airplane strapped to the bottom of the zeppelin for emergencies," said Indy. "I think we can safely call this one."

They were halfway down a passageway that they hoped was going in the right direction when a voice shouted, "Stop, spies! Or I shoot!"

Behind them a Gestapo agent was pulling a Luger out of his black leather trench coat. But he didn't get far with it. A screaming crewman slapped it out of his hand. A stray bullet would turn the zeppelin into a fireball.

"Time to get out of this gasbag while the getting is good," said Indy, sliding open a hatchway.

Below was the biplane, suspended on hooks. It looked very fragile. The metal ladder leading to it looked very narrow.

"Do we have to?" Henry shouted above the zeppelin engines and the howling wind.

"Do we have a choice?" Indy shouted back.

◆　　　◆　　　◆

"We must be well out of German airspace by now and close to the Mediterranean," Henry said. He was in the back seat of the biplane, while Indy worked the controls. "Congratulations, Junior. I didn't know you could fly."

"Fly, yes," Indy said. "Land, no." Then he added, "But maybe I won't have to."

Two planes were bearing down on them. Messerschmitts. The most deadly fighter-bombers in the Nazi air force.

"Indy!" Henry shouted. "Why are we slowing down?"

"They're too fast for us," said Indy. "But maybe they're too fast for their own good too."

He was right. The warplanes zoomed past. They were a mile away before they could turn for another pass.

"This time I'll be ready for them," Henry vowed, fingering the machine gun mounted behind him. He cleared his throat. "Uhh, wonder how this works?"

"Pull back on the lever—then jerk the trigger!" Indy yelled, turning and pointing.

"Right," Henry said as the Messerschmitts came back.

The machine gun went off. Henry looked like he was riding a bucking bronco. Then the gun smoke lifted, and he saw that he had scored a direct hit—on the biplane's tail.

"Whoops," he said, then shouted to Indy, "Son, I'm sorry. They got us."

"No sweat. We've still got somewhere to go," Indy said. He gulped. "Down."

Indy spotted a blacktop road below. Perfect spot for a landing, if only he knew how.

"Can't be so hard," he said, nosing the plane down.

The plane hit the asphalt, the wheel struts snapping. The craft went skidding out of control on its belly, until it came to a crashing stop in the parking lot of a roadside tavern.

Indy leaped out of the cockpit, followed by his father. He found himself facing a man staring at them open-mouthed, frozen in shock, with one hand on the car door he was in the middle of opening.

"Want to trade in your old heap for a spiffy plane?" asked Indy. "Great deal. A little body-work and it'll be as good as new."

Without giving the man a chance to answer, Indy elbowed past him and got behind the wheel. His father jumped in beside him. A moment later Indy and Henry were roaring down the road, with the man still staring after them, and with a Messerschmitt, machine guns blazing, closing in on them overhead.

All Henry could say was, "Head for Princeton!"

But Indy spotted something better. A tunnel. Their car made it. The Messerschmitt didn't. Both its wings ripped off as it entered the tunnel. Its body turned into a flaming hulk passing over the car.

"We did it!" Indy exulted. Then he said, "Uh-oh."

The flaming plane had fallen like a spent bullet to block the tunnel exit. Indy gritted his teeth. The car shot through the exploding mass of fire and flying metal.

"They don't come any closer than that," Henry said as they came out of the tunnel.

80

"Yes they do," said Indy. He saw a bomb from the second Messerschmitt dropping in their path.

Using all his muscle, Indy sent the car into a two-wheeled swerve—through a guardrail. The car bounced down an embankment, then came to a soft landing.

"Sand, beautiful sand," Indy said, as he and his father emerged shakily from the smoldering car onto a sunlit beach.

"The Mediterranean, mother of civilization," said Henry, looking out at the gleaming sea.

"What a picture. Just us, the sand, the sea, the sun, and about a million gulls," said Indy, looking at the birds that covered the beach. Then he said, "Oh yeah, one thing more. That second Messerschmitt."

The Messerschmitt was coming in low over the sea. They were right in its gunsights. The pilot was holding his fire until he couldn't miss. They were as good as dead.

Indy didn't blame his father for turning and running. But why was Henry screaming and waving his arms? Then Indy saw the panicked gulls rise in a vast cloud into the plane's path, blocking its sights and clogging its engines.

As the plane crashed into the sea, Henry said, "I just remembered a quotation from

Charlemagne: 'Let my armies be the rocks and the trees and birds in the sky.'"

Indy grinned. "You scholars. Save that stuff for Brody, when we catch up with him in Iskenderun."

◆　　　◆　　　◆

Indy's grin was even bigger a week later, when he saw an old friend waiting on the Iskenderun train platform.

"Sallah," Indy said. "Long time, no see. How are things back in Cairo? Still digging up interesting stuff?"

"Not as interesting as when you were around," Sallah said.

"Sallah is the best digger in Egypt," Indy told his father. "He was a great help to me on that little trip I took there."

"Oh yes, I heard rumors about that," Henry said. "Some kind of wild-goose chase after a so-called Lost Ark."

Sallah started to protest, but Indy silenced him with a look.

"Right," Indy said. "Can't win them all. But the Grail is one chase we *are* going to win. Sallah, take us to Marcus and we'll be on our way."

Sallah sadly shook his head. "Too late, my friend. The Germans got here first. They have Marcus. They have the map. And they are on their way to get the Grail."

Chapter 8

"THE NAZIS CAME IN FORCE," SAID INDY, PEER-
ing through binoculars. He was crouched with
his father and Sallah behind a large rock at the
foothills of the mountains. They had beaten the
Germans over the desert with the help of a
shortcut Sallah knew and a battered auto he
had borrowed from a brother-in-law.

Indy saw troop carriers loaded with German
soldiers emerging from rising dust in the distance. Then he saw horses and camels bearing
native mercenaries; supply trucks; an open car
carrying Vogel, Donovan, Elsa, and Marcus; and
a tank with cannons fore and aft. Indy had a

strong hunch that the tank was serving as a prison for Brody.

"They grabbed Marcus on the streets of Iskenderun," Sallah said. "They bribed the authorities. I couldn't stop them."

"That's okay," said Indy. "We've got them where we want them now." Then he ducked as the tank cannon flashed and a shell whistled over their heads.

Behind them, their parked auto exploded.

"I could have sworn we were out of range," Indy said. "They must have spotted the sun glinting on the field glasses."

Sallah looked at the car wreckage. "My brother-in-law will kill me," he groaned.

"If the Nazis don't do it first," said Indy, squinting through the glasses. "They're coming after us."

The Nazi column had split itself in two. Most of them, led by Donovan and Elsa in the auto, continued toward the mountains. A smaller detachment, led by the tank with Vogel in command, was coming to check out the burning car.

"I'm sure now that Marcus is in the tank," Indy said. "It's the perfect spot to hold him as a hostage in case of trouble."

"We have to save him," said Henry fiercely.

"Cool it, Dad," Indy said. "I know he's an old pal. But no sense taking foolish risks."

"How can *you* say *that*?" his father asked.

Indy shrugged. "I'm young and crazy. You're supposed to be old and wise."

From behind the boulder they watched the Nazis arrive. Vogel got out of the tank with the crew, all of them holding guns at the ready, and inspected the remains of the car. He was disgusted to find no corpses.

"They're still alive," he said to an aide. "And they've got guns!" he yelled, diving for the ground as shots rang out.

"Who the—?" Indy wondered. Then he saw figures rising from among the rocks and charging the Nazis. He recognized the man in the lead—Kazim. Indy shuddered as Kazim and his followers were cut down by a hail of Nazi bullets.

"A brave guy, willing to give his life to defend the Grail—but a suicide charge," muttered Indy. He turned to his father. "See what I meant about foolish risks—?"

But Henry was no longer there. Taking advantage of the distraction, he had run for the tank and climbed in through the turret. But before he could sneak out with Marcus, the firefight was over.

"Dad's trapped. Let's move it," Indy said as Vogel and his crew climbed back into the tank.

Sallah flashed a smile. "Hey. Just like old times."

Both of them broke cover and dashed to the place where native mercenaries had tethered their horses. Indy leaped onto one, Sallah onto another. They scattered the rest, then raced off in opposite directions, making sure the tank spotted them first.

The tank didn't hesitate. It headed after Indy. Vogel knew for sure whose scalp he wanted most.

Following the tank, a pair of troop carriers packed with soldiers took up the chase as well.

With shells exploding around him, Indy wheeled the horse around and cut between the tank and the troop carriers. The tank turret revolved as the cannon tracked him, blasting away.

"Here goes nothing," Indy said to himself, and brought his horse to a dead halt. The cannon stopped moving, took dead aim, and fired.

"Perfect," Indy said as his horse moved aside and the cannon shell blew one of the troop carriers to pieces.

But the cannon was turning on him again, ready to fire.

"Here goes *some*thing," muttered Indy. He charged the tank, jumped from the saddle onto it, and straddling the gun barrel, jammed a piece of rock into its mouth.

There was a muffled explosion as the cannon backfired. Smoke billowed out of the turret hatchway when it was thrown open.

Indy, though, didn't see Vogel climb out of it, with fury gleaming in smoke-reddened eyes and a long length of chain in his hands. Indy was too busy knocking off soldiers like ninepins as they clambered awkwardly from the other troop carrier onto the tank after him. Indy wasn't aware of Vogel's being behind him until the soldiers were out for the count, and Vogel's chain was around his neck.

"Die, American dog," snarled Vogel, tightening it.

"Hey, who writes your dialogue, anyway?" said Indy as he managed to turn enough to get his hands around Vogel's neck.

"That's the way, Junior!" he heard Henry

shout as he and Brody emerged from the turret. They had teamed inside the tank to take care of the crew, Brody with his flying fists, Henry with his squirting fountain pen.

Sallah played his part on the team now, as well, riding up on his horse beside the tank.

"You're heading straight for a cliff!" he shouted. "Jump for it! Quick!"

Brody leaped from the tank and made a neat three-point landing on the back of Sallah's horse.

Vogel tried to jump too, when he saw that Sallah was telling the truth. The tank was speeding toward a steep cliff dead ahead, as if drawn by a lethal magnet.

Indy dove to stop him, grabbing him by the ankle. He succeeded—but at a terrible cost.

In the struggle to break free Vogel flailed out with his free foot—and sent Indy's father flying. Henry went bouncing onto a tank tread, where he lay stunned. The tank—and certain death— moved toward his inert body.

"Go, baby!" Indy muttered through clenched teeth. Keeping one hand on Vogel's ankle, he used his other to lash out with his bullwhip. It curled around his father's ankle. The whip drew taut, and Henry was saved—for the moment.

Then Indy felt Vogel fighting to get free. He

needed two hands now. He tossed the whip handle to Sallah, who was still riding beside the tank. Sallah completed the rescue, easing Henry off the tread to roll gently out of the tank's path.

Brushing himself off, Henry got to his feet, none the worse for wear. But he felt sick at what he saw.

Indy and Vogel had become tangled together in Vogel's chain. When the tank reached the cliff, they both leaped for their lives, but the chain stayed hooked to the tank. Though he struggled desperately to free himself, Indy could not. He was dragged over the edge of the cliff with Vogel and the tank.

Henry, Marcus, and Sallah ran to the cliff edge. The tank lay shattered far below.

"I'm sorry," Marcus said, putting his hand on Henry's shoulder.

"Now *that* was close," said a voice behind them.

Indy looked a bit dazed. With one hand he had to hold up his pants, which had been ripped to shreds when he had wriggled out of the chain to grab a protruding rock on his way down. But otherwise he was intact.

"I thought I had lost you, Junior," Henry said.

"I thought you had too," Indy admitted.

"Junior?" said Sallah.

"That's his name," Henry said proudly. "Henry Jones, *Junior*."

"I like Indiana," Indy said.

"We named the *dog* Indiana," Henry said.

At this point Indy was glad to be able to say, "I hate to change the subject, but we still have work to do."

He pointed to the north, where a gigantic explosion was blasting a mountain apart.

◆   ◆   ◆

"Looks like Donovan and Elsa have found the canyon of the Crescent Moon by going through the mountain—just like the inscription on the stone said," Indy observed.

He and the others had galloped on horseback over the desert to reach the site of the explosion. The blast had ripped open the mountain to reveal a narrow canyon.

"But they won't get much farther," said Marcus. "They don't have a clue to the dangers awaiting them when they try to get their hands on the Grail. As soon as they fail and go away, we can make our move."

"We're like the four heroes of the Grail legend," agreed Henry, his eyes shining. "Sallah is like Bors, the ordinary man. Marcus is like

Perceval, the holy Innocent. I am like Lancelot, the old crusader who was father of the knight who finally succeeded. And Galahad—that's you, Junior."

Indy grimaced. "I don't even know what the Grail looks like."

"Nobody does," said Henry. "The one who is worthy will."

"I hope that leaves out the Nazis," said Indy. "Let's go find out how they're doing."

Cautiously they rode through the narrow canyon, and then out into a vast space dominated by a huge temple built into the mountainside.

"The Temple of the Sun," said Henry in awe.

"Our friends are already inside," said Indy. There were several empty German vehicles parked at the foot of the steps that led to the temple entranceway of giant columns. "Come on."

The others followed him into the temple. From the interior came the sound of angry orders being shouted. When they peered into the central courtyard, they saw why.

The headless corpses of two native mercenaries lay on the ground. Donovan was commanding a third native, at gunpoint, to enter a dark passageway. Terrified, the man refused—

until a savage prod from Donovan's pistol sent the man forward. There was a whooshing noise. The man fell backward, minus his head, to join the other victims.

"The first booby trap," said Indy, going over the diary warnings in his mind.

"Trouble is, looks like we're in a trap ourselves," said Henry.

Indy turned to see a pair of Nazi soldiers pointing pistols at them.

Donovan's face lit up like a child seeing Santa when Indy and the others were herded before him.

Elsa's face, though, grew pale.

"I never expected to see you again," she said to Indy.

"I keep turning up, like a bad penny," Indy said.

"Nonsense," said Donovan, smiling. "You're very valuable. You're the one who can find the Grail. What do you say? Want to go down in history?"

"As what?" said Indy. "A Nazi stooge like you?"

"The Nazis," said Donovan scornfully. "They merely seek the Grail as a trophy, a symbol of supremacy to cow the world they want to conquer. I want the Grail for what it can give—everlasting life. I'll be drinking my own health when Hitler has gone the way of the dodo."

"Don't count on finding it, if you're counting on me to help you," said Indy. He grinned when Donovan pulled out his pistol. "What are you going to do, shoot me? That won't get you anywhere."

"You know something? You're absolutely right," said Donovan. Then he leveled his gun and fired.

With horror Indy saw his father double over.

Marcus, kneeling beside Henry, said, "Unless we do something, he's a goner."

"Donovan, get him a doctor," said Indy, holding his groaning father in his arms and looking up with hatred at Donovan's smirking face.

"He's beyond the help of doctors," Donovan said. "The only thing that can save him is the healing power of the Grail. The Grail that you will get for us. Well, Indiana Jones, is it yes or no? Make up your mind fast. Because for your father, it's now or never."

Chapter 9

"HANG ON, DAD," INDY SAID, BENDING OVER HIS father. "I'll be back in a jiffy—with the Grail."

With a trembling hand Henry gestured for Indy to bend close, so that Donovan and Elsa couldn't hear his rasping whisper. "The diary . . . your only guide . . . your one hope."

Indy nodded. He had thought of that already.

At the entrance to the passageway, he pulled out the diary and read: "The challenges will number three. First, the Breath of God, only the penitent man will pass. Second, the Word of God, only in the footsteps of God will he proceed. Third, the Path of God, only in the leap from the lion's head will he prove his worth."

The Breath of God? The penitent man? It made no sense.

But when he entered the passageway, it suddenly did.

He heard a hissing noise. Like a sinner humbling himself before the Almighty, he dropped to his knees—just in time to dodge a blade that swung like a pendulum across the spot where his neck would have been. Its breeze felt like the chill breath of death passing through his hair.

"Close shave," he muttered as he jammed the mechanism of the blade so that it wouldn't get him when he returned.

The next clue was far easier. *The Word of God.* In olden times, that would be "Jehovah." And when Indy entered a small chamber and looked down at its cobblestoned floor, he saw what to do.

Each cobblestone had a different letter carved into it. He found the one with the letter "J" and stepped on it.

"Oops," he said, as his foot went down into the hole that suddenly appeared. He pulled it up just in time to avoid getting bitten by an evil-looking, giant black spider.

He slapped himself on the forehead. "Of course. In Latin, Jehovah begins with an 'I.' "

One by one he stepped on the letters of the Latin spelling: I-E-H-O-V-A.

First prize in the spelling bee, thought Indy as a wall moved aside and he stepped into another passageway. "Now where's 'the lion's head' I'm supposed to leap from?"

The end of the passageway was draped in cobwebs. Indy brushed them aside and stared up at a giant stone lion's head jutting out from a rock wall. The head looked out over a huge abyss that Indy had to cross.

Indy climbed up onto the lion's head.

"I'm supposed to jump from *here* to *there*?" Indy muttered. He saw the jagged rocks at the bottom of the abyss, and how far it was to the other side. He calculated his chances of making it there. "No way."

The trouble was, it was the only way. The only way to get to the Grail. The only way to save his father.

Indy shrugged. "It has to be a test of faith. Well, I guess you gotta believe." And gathering all his strength, he made the big leap.

"Big mistake," he groaned as he saw he was falling short. Then his feet hit solid ground. "What the—?"

He looked down and shook his head in admiration at what an artist had done long ago.

The ground beneath his feet had been painted to look like the rocks far below. Only when he stood on it did he realize the deception.

"That's the last of the riddles," he said, spotting a passageway ahead. "Now for the payoff. The Grail."

But when he entered the tall-columned courtyard beyond the passageway, he saw not one Grail, but a vast array of them. They were a vast array of all shapes and sizes, and for a moment he was blinded by the dazzle of precious metals and jewels. Then he saw something else gleaming brightly—a knight in armor heading toward him, with a monstrous sword raised high in his hands.

Indy had no time to dodge, just time to say, "Oh, no—"

But the sword never struck home. When the knight raised it higher, its weight toppled him over so that he lay helpless, like a turtle on its back.

"I knew you would come," said the knight. "But my strength has left me."

"Who are you?" said Indy, though he knew the answer.

"The last of the three brothers who swore an oath to guard the Grail," said the knight. "I was chosen to stay here because I was the bravest and most worthy. The honor was mine until another came to challenge me in single combat." He picked up the sword and extended it toward Indy. "I pass this to you who vanquished me, though I see you have a curious weapon of your own."

He gave a puzzled look at the bullwhip that hung from Indy's belt.

"Look, let me explain—" Indy began.

He didn't get a chance. A voice interrupted him. Donovan's voice.

Donovan had entered the courtyard. Behind him came Elsa. And in Donovan's hand was a gun.

"Thanks for leading the way, Dr. Jones," Donovan said. "I knew you could do it. Now one last favor. Which of these many Cups is the right one?"

Indy shrugged. "Beats me. You're on your own, pal."

"Beware," the knight added. "Choose wisely. Just as the true Grail will bring you life, a false one will take it from you."

Donovan stared in bewilderment at the collection of chalices before him. But Elsa's eyes lit up instantly.

"I see it!" she exclaimed, and picked up a superbly wrought vessel adorned with exquisite precious stones.

Instantly Donovan grabbed it from her. "Of course. Anyone can see this is it. A cup for a King of Kings."

Donovan licked his lips as he dipped the chalice into the water of the courtyard fountain. His Adam's apple bobbed as he gulped it down. His eyes closed in ecstasy as he savored the taste of his triumph.

Then his eyes popped open. His body jerked in agony. His face twitched in uncontrollable spasms.

"What . . . is . . . happening . . . to . . . me?" he gasped.

Elsa saw what was happening to him, and turned her eyes away in horror. Indy forced himself to keep looking, though he felt a little sick.

Donovan had been a well-preserved middle-aged man. Now his body bent over, his face turned into a mass of wrinkles, and his hair and teeth disappeared.

His last words were, "No . . . no . . . no . . . no . . . no . . ."

Even as his final word died in the air, his skin

"I know you from books," said Henry. "But tell me, if you had the Grail, why have you aged so?"

"Many times my spirit faltered, and I was not worthy to drink from the cup," the knight explained. "Each time, I aged a year. But now at last I can die with honor. This brave knight-errant has come to take my place."

"Uh, there's a little misunderstanding here," said Indy.

"He is not a knight-errant," said Henry. "He is my errant son who has led an impure life."

"Right. Definitely impure," Indy agreed.

"Is it you then, brother?" the knight asked Henry.

"No, I am only a scholar," said Henry.

"You?" the knight asked Brody.

"Me?" said Brody. "Hardly. I display suits of armor, not wear them."

The knight turned to Sallah. "Ah. Good knight."

Sallah's English was good, but not that good. "Good night," he responded. "Sleep tight."

The knight was puzzled. "Then why have you come?"

"For this," Elsa said, grabbing the Grail. "We've got it, and now we can go."

"No," the knight declared. "The Grail can

never leave this place. Remaining here is the price of immortality."

"So you say," said Elsa. She turned to Indy. "It's ours. Yours and mine. Forever."

"Listen to the knight," warned Henry.

"Stop!" shouted Indy as Elsa gave him a last pleading look, turned, and ran for the exit.

"Don't cross the seal," the knight called after her.

But Elsa heard nothing, saw nothing—until her flying feet went over a metal seal on the floor before the exit. She froze then, as a thunderous sound filled the air.

"The temple! It's falling apart!" said Henry, dodging showers of debris.

"Got to get out of here quick," said Indy.

Elsa had the same idea. But she stumbled and fell as the ground beneath her feet gave a violent shudder. At the spot where the metal seal had been, the earth was splitting open.

"No!" she screamed as the Grail flew from her hands and rolled toward the edge of the widening abyss.

Indy led his father, Brody, and Sallah in jumping over the crack in the earth before it grew too large to keep them from the exit. But Elsa froze, straddling the chasm, transfixed by the sight of the Grail just out of her reach.

"Got to help her," said Indy. But before he could get to her, she had fallen into the crack and was clinging to its edge with both hands. Temptingly close to her, on a ledge of earth, was the Grail.

"Elsa!" Indy shouted as he reached out to pull her up.

But Elsa wasn't listening.

"I can reach it!" she said as her one hand strained to reach the Grail—and her other hand slipped inexorably away from Indy's.

"Indy!" she screamed as she plummeted downward.

But Indy couldn't save her—or himself.

The sudden weight of her fall had caught him off-balance and jerked him over the edge. Elsa was gone, and now he was the one dangling in the abyss, hanging on to the edge for dear life.

He suddenly felt two hands grasping both his wrists, and looked up to see his father.

"Quick, pull yourself up," Henry said. "I can't hold on much longer."

"Try, please try," gasped Indy. "The Grail. I can get it if I just—" He wrested one hand free and began to reach for the gleaming chalice.

"Indiana," his father said in a sharp voice.

Indy stopped. "Hey, you've never called me that before," he said.

"Indy, forget the Grail," Henry said. "Let it go."

Indy looked away from the Grail and up at his father.

"Right," Indy said, and with Henry's help he lifted himself out of the abyss. Then he and his father gave a parting wave to the knight, who stood amid the temple ruins, watching them depart.

Together they smiled when Marcus Brody mounted one of their waiting horses and shouted, "Indy, Henry, Sallah! Follow me! I know the way. Yahoo!"

Together they shook their heads when his horse went galloping in a circle and then headed for the horizon with Brody desperately clinging to the stirrups.

"Once got lost in his own museum," sighed Henry.

"Uh-huh," said Indy.

"Guess we have to go after him," said Henry.

"Guess we do," agreed Indy.

Father and son looked into each other's eyes, while Sallah brought them their horses. Neither of them had to say what they both were thinking.

They might have lost the Grail. But they wouldn't have traded it for what they had found.

"You first, Junior," said Henry after they had saddled up.

"Yes sir," said Indy as they rode off together into the unknown.